SPEEDBOAT RACE

Speedboat Race
Copyright © 2024 by Amir T. Khan

Published in the United States of America

Library of Congress Control Number: 2024914689
ISBN   Paperback: 979-8-89091-654-9
ISBN   eBook: 979-8-89091-655-6

All rights reserved. No part of this publication may be reproduced, stored in a retrieval system or transmitted in any way by any means, electronic, mechanical, photocopy, recording or otherwise without the prior permission of the author except as provided by USA copyright law.

The opinions expressed by the author are not necessarily those of ReadersMagnet, LLC.

ReadersMagnet, LLC
10620 Treena Street, Suite 230 | San Diego, California, 92131 USA
1.619. 354. 2643 | www.readersmagnet.com

Book design copyright © 2024 by ReadersMagnet, LLC. All rights reserved.

Cover design by Ericka Obando
Interior design by Daniel Lopez

SPEEDBOAT RACE

Written by **Amir T. Khan**

Illustrated by **Zoya & Zysha Khan**

DEDICATION

I dedicate this book to my wife Maira, daughters Zoya and Zysha, my parents Tariq and Rosario Khan, mother in-law Syeda Iffat, and siblings Jamil and Yasmin.

WHAT KIDS HAVE TO SAY

"What happens next, …good."
"I liked the drawings." — Drake B.

"I like the old and new illustrations.
It is so good." — Riyan B.

"Buy this book for me, I really like the pictures
and the ending part." — Jagger K.

"I learned that you should never give up.
Enjoyed this book." — Rayyan S

"I love this little boat story and would
read this story many more times."
— Aiyana D.

"I like this book and how he started in fourth place.
I would recommend this book for other 2nd graders
or older." — Marley P.

"I like that the author makes the book dramatic."
— Ayla B.

"I like to read this book and think other kids will like it too." — Alina B.

TABLE OF CONTENTS

DEDICATION v

ACKNOWLEDGMENTS xiii

CHAPTER 1: PREPARATION 1

CHAPTER 2: DRY RUN 5

CHAPTER 3: QUICK REPAIRS 9

CHAPTER 4: RACE DAY 11

APPENDIX: ORIGINAL 1990 ILLUSTRATIONS 17

YOUNG AUTHORS SEAL 23

ABOUT THE AUTHOR 25

ACKNOWLEDGMENTS

I want to thank Jeff Dometita for his support and feedback.

I want to thank fellow author and Northwestern University Alumnus Nick Kamboj for guidance on publishing and editing.

I want to thank my daughters Zoya and Zysha for their extraordinary illustrations.

Also, I would like to thank my parents Rosario and Tariq Khan support and for keeping the original manuscript.

Last, I want to thank my wife Maira for her support and inspiration.

CHAPTER 1
PREPARATION

It was a Tuesday, the day before the big speed boat race, and John was checking his boat for any cracks and scratches. He found only one scratch that he had to fix. It was not that bad, but John did not want to take a risk. He wanted his boat to be well prepared to win the race.

After fixing the speedboat, he went inside the house and studied the course map.

COURSE

JOHN LOOKING AT THE COURSE MAP.

He noticed the course was a bit difficult because of the sharp curves and turns. It started under a bridge and then went towards the middle of the lake. There were several turns right and left that were curved.

He decided to personally take a walk to the course after studying the map for a few minutes. Looking over the bridge he could observe everything much clearer. Following the initial starting markers, boats can speed into the open lake. That first open curve is what had John a little nervous. He would not want to crash with another boat right at the start. With big waves that would make it a very difficult turn right away.

BRIDGE

JOHN LOOKING OUT AT THE COURSE FROM THE BRIDGE.

Today's weather was sunny and partly cloudy with 3-knot winds. The waves were calm.

He could not resist the idea of trying the track before the race. He went back to get his boat and put it into the water.

LAUNCH

JOHN LAUNCHING HIS BOAT INTO THE WATER.

CHAPTER 2
DRY RUN

On his boat, he drove to the middle of the lake. With the course set, it was easier than looking at the map. Still, the course was a bit risky. Any mistake could lead the boat to crash with the adjacent walls of the bridge dock.

John rode the boat slowly and tried to find the best speed to get through the track.

PACE

JOHN PRACTICING AND PACING HIS BOAT.

After going around the track several times, he decided to park the boat and headed toward his truck.

He secured the boat to his truck and started to tow the boat home.

TOWING

JOHN TOWING HIS BOAT BACK HOME.

He did not realize that some kids were throwing heavy rocks near the loading docks. Unfortunately, it appears some rocks skipped and hit his boat.

He was very disappointed and worried that he would not be able to participate in the race tomorrow. Some of the dents were quite deep, and he realized that, even if he worked all night long, he would not be able to finish the job.

However, he did not want to give up his desire to win the race. He decided to fix the dents and started working on them right away.

CHAPTER 3
QUICK REPAIRS

First, he cut around some of the deep dents and straightened them with a hammer. Next, he pulled the others with a dent puller. He soldered the cuts back again and then leveled out with putty. Other holes he hammered, sanded, and painted. John also checked the engine to make sure there were no issues. He put a new fuel filter and topped off his fuel. By the time he finished maintaining, waxing, and buffing out, it was 3:00 am. He realized he only had five hours to sleep.

WORKBENCH

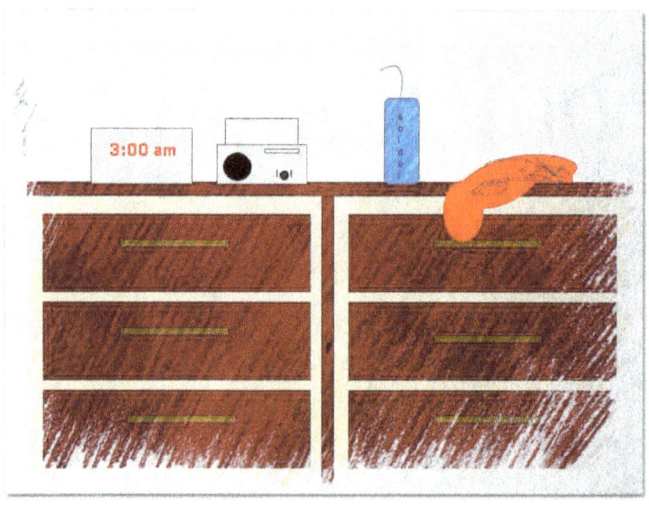

IT'S 3:00 AM ON THE CLOCK ON JOHN'S WORKBENCH.

CHAPTER 4
RACE DAY

The next morning, he woke up and, after a good breakfast, he left for the race site. He was very proud of his work. His boat looked new.

When he arrived at the lake, he noticed other racers were already in their boats and taking practice runs. He also put his boat in the water to take few practice turns.

Soon everyone lined up for the start of the race. At the sound of the gunfire, boats began to hit their throttles and race.

START

JOHN LINING UP TO START WITH THE OTHER RACERS.

John noticed that he was already behind four boats. He maneuvered his boat, but other riders did not give him enough room to bypass them.

John continued trying. At the next turn, he expertly turned the boat and passed two of the crafts. Now John was in third. He continued to maneuver his boat and was determined to win this race.

PASS

JOHN'S BOAT PASSING ANOTHER RACER.

Soon the race was in the open lake. Here John sped his boat masterfully and bypassed the next craft.

SECOND

JOHN IS NOW IN SECOND PLACE.

Now the race was between him and another boat whose driver was very famous and always won boat races.

At one point, John thought that he was going to lose the race. He was very disheartened, but then he thought of the hard work he put in last night to fix his boat.

Now there was only a quarter of a mile left. Still, there were two more curves before the finish line.

John decided to close the gap between him and the other boat. He got so close to the other vessel that he even was a bit scared but stayed close. Then there came a sharp curve. He slightly slowed his boat to get some room and then sharply sped up while turning the boat. He had practiced this turn several times yesterday. To his surprise, he was able to take the lead and win the race.

John was very proud of himself. He knew that he won this race because he did not give up.

He worked hard to repair his boat and practiced the course. It all paid off in winning first place.

FIRST

JOHN IS IN FIRST PLACE AND ABOUT TO WIN THE RACE.

John was ready to relax and enjoy his victory. He could not wait for next season to start.

TROPHY

JOHN'S NEW FIRST PLACE TROPHY ON HIS FIREPLACE MANTEL.

APPENDIX

ORIGINAL 1990 ILLUSTRATIONS BY AMIR

MAP OF THE COURSE

JOHN'S WORKBENCH AT 3:00 AM

JOHN PRACTICING AND PACING HIS BOAT

JOHN PRACTICING WITH OTHER RACERS BEFORE THE RACE.

JOHN PASSING THE LAST RACER TO WIN THE RACE.

JOHN'S NEW TROPHY ON THE FIREPLACE MANTEL

ILLINOIS YOUNG AUTHORS SEAL

ABOUT THE AUTHOR

In 1990, at age 12, Amir Khan created this fictional story while in 6th grade at Bannes Elementary school, IL. The school district selected Amir's story to represent it for 6th-grade submission to Illinois Young Authors Conference. It was a wonderful experience.

After many years, Amir's mom stored the original manuscript in a safe deposit box. She gave him the original manuscript for his 40th birthday.

In hopes that this story will inspire young authors to pursue and create their own stories, Amir was motivated to publish this simple work and share it with the world.

Currently, Amir works in Information Technology. He has a Bachelor's in Computer Science from Northern Illinois University and a Master's in Computer Information Systems from Northwestern University. Amir is also an adjunct professor teaching technology at the collegiate level. He hopes to author future stories in fiction and nonfiction.

Thank you for your support, I hope you enjoyed this wonderful story, please leave a review:

www.ingramcontent.com/pod-product-compliance
Lightning Source LLC
LaVergne TN
LVHW020416070526
838199LV00054B/3637